Naptime, Laptime

To my own dear grandma, Philomena,
and to her sisters Aunt Mary and Aunt Jussie,
who held me in their laps

—E.S.

To my friend, Elizabeth

—M.S.

ISBN 0-439-35963-5

Text copyright © 1995 by Eileen Spinelli.
Illustrations copyright © 1995 by Melissa Sweet.
All rights reserved.
Published by Scholastic Inc.
SCHOLASTIC, CARTWHEEL BOOKS, and associated logos are
trademarks and/or registered trademarks of Scholastic Inc.

12 11 10 9 8 7 6 5 4 3 2   1 2 3 4 5 6/0

Printed in the U.S.A.   08

First Scholastic paperback printing, November 2001

Naptime, Laptime

by Eileen Spinelli
Illustrated by Melissa Sweet

SCHOLASTIC INC.

New York Toronto London Auckland Sydney
Mexico City New Delhi Hong Kong Buenos Aires

Birds bed down in a cozy nest

A cave is where bears like to rest

A patch of leaves suits three small mice

And seals like snoozing on the ice

Cows slumber in an old red barn

And kittens, in a bowl of yarn

A pig flops down with a splash and a thud
To dream her dreams in squishy mud

A dog likes dozing in a chair

While fleas nod off in doggie's hair

And if, indeed, sharks fall asleep

It must be someplace dark and deep

A lion lolls in jungle gloom

An elephant needs a lot of room

Koalas cuddle in a tree

Skunks sleep in strictest privacy

A snake may drowse upon a rock

A spider, in the kitchen clock

But there's no better place to nap
Than right here on my grandma's lap.